Makenzie
& Friends

By Denisha Branch

Illustrated By Cameron Wilson

MAKENZIE AND FRIENDS
By: Denisha Branch

All rights reserved 2020. Except for brief excerpts for review purposes, no part of this book may be reproduced or used in any form without written permission from Denisha Branch.

This document is published by Denisha Branch located in the United States of America. It is protected by the United States Copyright Act, all applicable state laws and international copyright laws. The information in this document is accurate to the best of the ability of Denisha Branch at the time of writing. The content of this document is subject to change without notice.

ISBN-13: Paperback
9781657189874

Dedication

I would like to dedicate this book to my daughter, my late mother, grandmother and all of my family♥

My name is Makenzie and I have friends from all places.

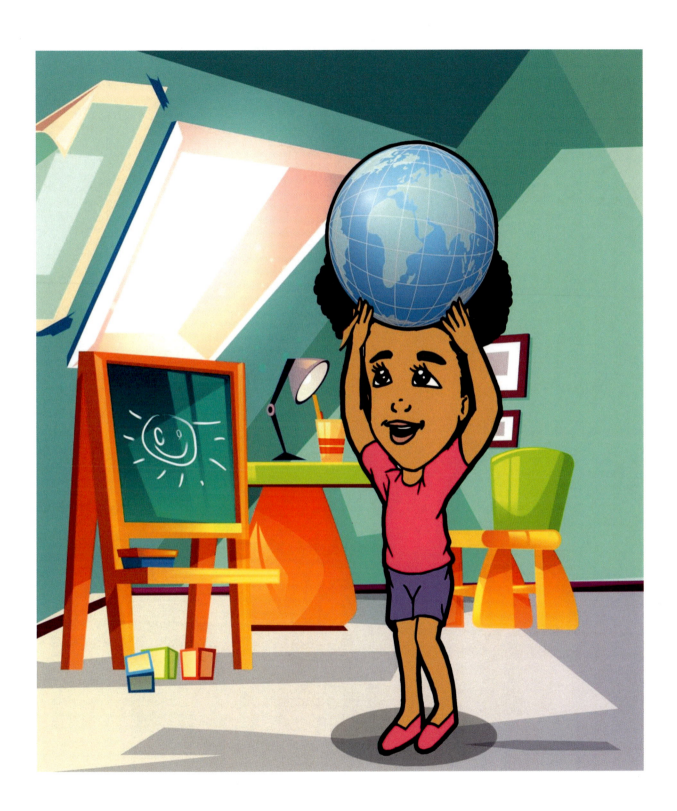

When we are together,
we make silly faces.

We always greet each other in our native tongue. As this is the language spoken when we first begun.

Hola, I am Juan and
I'm from Spain.

Konnichiwa, my name is Aiko I'm from Japan.

Bonjour, my name is Emma and I'm from France.

My friends are the best and we always get alone.

We don't bite, we don't kick.

But we love to sing songs
(la, la, laaaaaa).

When in school our teachers tell us to always use our words, like "please, thank you, and do you see the little birds (tweet tweet)?"

We learn to count our numbers like 1, 2, 3. We also learn our letters like A, B, C.

So, you see me and my friends may be from different places. But we learn, smile, and love to make silly faces.

I truly love my friends,
they are close to my heart.
And when we get older, may
we never grow apart.

But wait there's more
you may want to explore ....
Without your support there
would be no us for sure.
Thank you _____ for being
our new friend.

About the Author

Denisha Branch also known as Luv Nisha was raised in Raeford, North Carolina. She is a motivational speaker, author, and entrepreneur. As an advocate for "Self Love", Denisha believes it is imperative that we teach our children to embrace who they are and also embrace those around them. She's set out to change the world one child at a time, one book at a time, and one speech at time. Making the world a better place through love is her ultimate goal.

The End.

Made in the USA
Columbia, SC
03 June 2020